A Note to Parents and Caregivers:

Read-it! Readers are for children who are just starting on the amazing road to reading. These beautiful books support both the acquisition of reading skills and the love of books.

The PURPLE LEVEL presents basic topics and objects using high frequency words and simple language patterns.

The RED LEVEL presents familiar topics using common words and repeating sentence patterns.

The BLUE LEVEL presents new ideas using a larger vocabulary and varied sentence structure.

The YELLOW LEVEL presents more challenging ideas, a broad vocabulary, and wide variety in sentence structure.

The GREEN LEVEL presents more complex ideas, an extended vocabulary range, and expanded language structures.

The ORANGE LEVEL presents a wide range of ideas and concepts using challenging vocabulary and complex language structures.

When sharing a book with your child, read in short stretches, pausing often to talk about the pictures. Have your child turn the pages and point to the pictures and familiar words. And be sure to reread favorite stories or parts of stories.

There is no right or wrong way to share books with children. Find time to read with your child, and pass on the legacy of literacy.

Adria F. Klein, Ph.D.
Professor Emeritus
California State University
San Bernardino, California

Editor: Jacqueline A. Wolfe
Designer: Nathan Gassman
Page Production: Angela Kilmer
Creative Director: Keith Griffin
Editorial Director: Carol Jones
The illustrations in this book were created digitally.

Picture Window Books
5115 Excelsior Boulevard
Suite 232
Minneapolis, MN 55416
877-845-8392
www.picturewindowbooks.com

Printed in the United States of America.

Library of Congress Cataloging-in-Publication Data
Jones, Christianne C.
The lifeguard / by Christianne C. Jones ; illustrated by Matthew Skeens.
p. cm. — (Read-it! readers)
ISBN 1-4048-1584-8 (hard cover)
[1. A rambunctious child complains that the lifeguard is spoiling his fun until his little
sister gets into trouble in the water. 2. Swimming—Safety measures—Fiction.
3. Lifeguards—Fiction.] I. Skeens, Matthew, ill. II. Title. III. Series.
PZ7.J6823Lif 2005
[E]—dc22   2005023157

The Lifeguard

by Christianne C. Jones
illustrated by Matthew Skeens

Special thanks to our advisers for their expertise:

Adria F. Klein, Ph.D.
Professor Emeritus, California State University
San Bernardino, California

Susan Kesselring, M.A.
Literacy Educator
Rosemount–Apple Valley–Eagan (Minnesota) School District

PICTURE WINDOW BOOKS
Minneapolis, Minnesota

I go to the pool every day in the summer.

My little sister comes, too.

6

There is just one problem.
The lifeguards are so mean!

8

They are always blowing their
whistles and yelling.

I dive into the pool.
The whistle blows.

"No diving in the shallow end," says a lifeguard.

I splash my little sister.
The whistle blows.

"No splashing other people,"
says a lifeguard.

I run and jump into the water.
The whistle blows.

"No running," says a lifeguard.

I push my friend into the pool.
The whistle blows.

"No pushing,"
says a lifeguard.

I eat some popcorn by the pool.
The whistle blows.

"No eating
on the deck,"
says a lifeguard.

19

The lifeguards always ruin my fun.

21

I know! I'll try to hide from the lifeguards.

I swim to the deep end.

My little sister follows me.

Oh, no! She can't touch the bottom!

I pull her to the edge of the pool.

The lifeguards climbs off their stands.

"Thanks for helping," they say.

I guess the lifeguards aren't so mean.

Maybe I'll be a lifeguard when I grow up.

More *Read-it!* Readers

Bright pictures and fun stories help you practice your reading skills. Look for more books at your level.

At the Beach 1-4048-0651-2
Bears on Ice 1-4048-1577-5
The Bossy Rooster 1-4048-0051-4
Dust Bunnies 1-4048-1168-0
Flying with Oliver 1-4048-1583-X
Frog Pajama Party 1-4048-1170-2
Galen's Camera 1-4048-1610-0
Jack's Party 1-4048-0060-3
Mike's Night-light 1-4048-1726-3
Nate the Dinosaur 1-4048-1728-X
The Playground Snake 1-4048-0556-7
Recycled! 1-4048-0068-9
Robin's New Glasses 1-4048-1587-2
The Sassy Monkey 1-4048-0058-1
Tuckerbean 1-4048-1591-0
What's Bugging Pamela? 1-4048-1189-3

Looking for a specific title or level? A complete list of *Read-it!* Readers is available on our Web site:

www.picturewindowbooks.com